Androcles and the Lion

by Sue Graves and Alex Paterson

W
FRANKLIN WATTS
LONDON•SYDNEY

Long ago, in Rome, there lived a slave called Androcles. He worked hard all day long. But his master was a cruel, mean man. He gave Androcles very little food and drink, and never let him rest at all. Androcles was very unhappy.

One day, Androcles decided to run away.
He waited for his master to go out, then
grabbed his few belongings and ran!

Androcles ran deeper and deeper into the forest, until he found a cave to hide in.

He found a few wild berries to eat,

and sipped ice-cold water from a small stream.

But although Androcles was glad to escape
from his cruel master, he was still tired
and still hungry.

One day, Androcles heard a terrible noise outside the cave. It made him tremble with fear.

It sounded like weeping and wailing.

Then moaning and groaning.

It got louder and louder and louder.

Androcles saw a shadow on the wall of the cave. It was getting bigger and bigger. Something was coming inside.

To his horror, Androcles saw it was a lion!

And it was making a terrible roaring sound.

The lion approached him, its roars getting louder and louder still. Androcles gulped. There was no way to escape. He was trapped!

The lion went up to Androcles. But it did not attack him. It just sat down and held up its paw. Androcles looked closely at it. The paw was red and swollen, and a large thorn was sticking out of it.

"So that's why you were roaring," said Androcle

"I can help you," said Androcles, kindly.

Carefully, he pulled out the thorn

and washed the wound. The lion licked

Androcles' hand. They looked at each other for

a few moments, smiling. The lion

turned around and left the cave.

For many years, Androcles lived happily in the forest. One day some soldiers arrived. They were looking for runaway slaves.

Now Androcles was in trouble!

Where could he hide? Before he could make a plan, the soldiers burst into the cave and took him prisoner.

The soldiers took Androcles to Rome.

They threw him into a cell.

You will be taken to the big arena,"

explained a soldier.

"There you will be thrown to the lions."

"That will teach you to run away from your master," laughed another soldier.

Androcles was scared.

How could he fight a lion?

He would surely be eaten!

The next day, Androcles was led into the arena.

It was vast. People were sitting all around.

The crowds were clapping and cheering,

waiting excitedly for the show to begin.

Then, the Emperor of Rome slowly raised

his hand. The clapping and cheering stopped.

A lion entered the arena. It walked round and round Androcles. The crowd gasped and Androcles shut his eyes, waiting for the lion to attack.

But, to the crowd's amazement, the lion licked him. Androcles opened his eyes in surprise. It was the same lion that he had helped in the cave, long ago!

The Emperor called Androcles over to him.

"Why didn't the lion attack you?" he asked.

"A long time ago, I helped this lion when

it was hurt," Androcles explained.

"Such kindness deserves a reward,"

said the Emperor, smiling. "You are now

a free man, Androcles. You will never be

a slave again."

The crowd clapped and cheered and stamped their feet.

"And you, Lion," added the Emperor, "will also be free. You may go to the forest to live in peace."

The crowd clapped and cheered and stamped their feet even louder.

So Androcles and the lion went back to the forest ... and both lived happily ever after.

Story order

Look at these 5 pictures and captions.
Put the pictures in the right order
to retell the story.

1

A lion enters the cave!

2

Androcles escapes from his master.

3

The soldiers capture Androcles.

4

The lion recognises Androcles.

5

Androcles helps the wounded lion.

Independent Reading

This series is designed to provide an opportunity for your child to read on their own. These notes are written for you to help your child choose a book and to read it independently.

In school, your child's teacher will often be using reading books which have been banded to support the process of learning to read. Use the book band colour your child is reading in school to help you make a good choice. *Androcles and the Lion* is a good choice for children reading at White Band in their classroom to read independently.

The aim of independent reading is to read this book with ease, so that your child enjoys the story and relates it to their own experiences.

About the book

The slave Androcles is desperate to escape his cruel master. He runs away to the forest and finds a cave to hide in. One day, a wounded lion comes inside. Androcles helps the lion get better. Much later, the lion may be able to help Androcles in return.

Before reading

Help your child to learn how to make good choices by asking:
"Why did you choose this book? Why do you think you will enjoy it?"
Ask your child about what they know about stories set in Ancient Rome. Then look at the cover with your child and ask: "What is the setting of this story? What does the character's name tell you?"
Remind your child that they can sound out the letters or groups of syllables to make a word if they get stuck.
Decide together whether your child will read the story independently or read it aloud to you.

During reading

Remind your child of what they know and what they can do independently. If reading aloud, support your child if they hesitate or ask for help by telling the word. If reading to themselves, remind your child that they can come and ask for your help if stuck.

After reading

Support comprehension by asking your child to tell you about the story. Use the story order puzzle to encourage your child to retell the story in the right sequence, in their own words. The correct sequence can be found on the next page.

Help your child think about the messages in the book that go beyond the story and ask: "Why did Androcles feel he had to run away? Why do you think he helped the lion? Why do you think the Emperor let him go free?"

Give your child a chance to respond to the story: "Have you ever helped someone and later they have helped you back? How did it make you feel?"

Extending learning

Help your child predict other possible outcomes of the story by asking: "If Androcles had not helped the lion, what might have happened? Do you think he still would have found his freedom? Why/why not?"

In the classroom, your child's teacher may be teaching recognition of recurring literary language in stories and traditional tales. The story contains several examples you can look at together such as:
"One day", "long ago", "for many years" and "happily ever after".
Find these examples in the story, think about how they help to help structure the story and are often used to begin or end sentences.

Franklin Watts
First published in Great Britain in 2018
by The Watts Publishing Group

Copyright © The Watts Publishing Group 2018
All rights reserved.

Series Editors: Jackie Hamley and Melanie Palmer
Series Advisors: Dr Sue Bodman and Glen Franklin
Series Designer: Peter Scoulding

A CIP catalogue record for this book is
available from the British Library.

ISBN 978 1 4451 6242 3 (hbk)
ISBN 978 1 4451 6263 8 (pbk)
ISBN 978 1 4451 6262 1 (library ebook)

Printed in China

Franklin Watts
An imprint of
Hachette Children's Group
Part of The Watts Publishing Group
Carmelite House
50 Victoria Embankment
London EC4Y 0DZ

An Hachette UK Company
www.hachette.co.uk

www.franklinwatts.co.uk

Answer to Story order: 2, 1, 5, 3, 4